A Marc Brown ARTHUR Chapter Book

Arthur Rocks with BINKY

Text by Stephen Krensky

Based on the teleplay by Sandra Willard

Little, Brown and Company

Boston   New York   London

For my mom, Renita

First Edition

The characters and events portrayed in this book are fictitious. Any
similarity to real persons, living or dead, is coincidental and not intended
by the author.

Arthur® is a registered trademark of Marc Brown.
Text has been reviewed and assigned a reading level by Laurel S. Ernst,
M.A., Teachers College, Columbia University, New York, New York;
reading specialist, Chappaqua, New York

ISBN 0-316-10422-1 (pb)

Library of Congresss Catalog Card Number 98-66440

10 9 8 7 6 5 4 3 2 1

WOR (HC)
COM-MO (PB)

Printed in the United States of America

Chapter 1

• • • • • • • • • • •

"How long has it been?" Buster asked.

He was standing in front of the Elwood City Civic Auditorium. He was not alone. Hundreds and hundreds of people were standing there with him. Among them were the Brain, Prunella, Rubella, Francine, and Francine's mother, Mrs. Frensky.

"We arrived at 11:05," said the Brain. "It's now 1:23. That's 138 minutes. Or in seconds, it's—"

"We get the picture," said Francine. "It's been a long time."

They were all waiting in line for BINKY

tickets to go on sale. BINKY was the hottest rock group to break out in weeks. There were BINKY posters, BINKY buttons, even BINKY toothbrushes. One radio station was planning a weekend where the songs would be all-BINKY, all the time.

Francine's mother looked toward the head of the line. "We're pretty far back," she said. "I hope we can get tickets."

"Don't worry, Mom," said Francine. "The Brain has it all figured out."

"He does?"

The Brain nodded. "This auditorium seats 7,025 people." He glanced at the line in front of them. "I'd say there are perhaps 350 people ahead of us. So that leaves 6,675 seats free."

"It's amazing how you can do all that figuring without a calculator," said Mrs. Frensky. "I guess they don't call you the Brain for nothing."

Rubella was sitting on the sidewalk

looking at some papers covered with drawings. "It's not just getting tickets that's important," she said, looking up. "It's getting the *right* tickets."

"What does that mean?" asked Buster. He was nervous enough already.

Rubella pointed to her papers. "I cast astrological charts for each of us."

"Why?" asked Buster.

"So we'll know where to sit. According to my calculations, we should avoid rows *K*, *O*, and *LL*."

"What difference will it make what row we're in?" asked Prunella.

"Because we want to increase our chances of catching stuff the group may throw into the crowd," said Francine.

The Brain looked down at Rubella's drawings. "I don't believe there's a scientific basis to support your approach."

Rubella just smiled at him. "It can't hurt," she said.

"None of this is going to help Arthur if he doesn't get here soon," said Francine. "His mom was supposed to drop him off." She looked at her watch. "But that was a while ago."

Buster shook his head. "He's never going to get good tickets at this rate."

"Can't we just buy a ticket for him?" asked Prunella. "I'm sure he'd pay us back later."

"It's not allowed," said Francine's mother. "The newspaper ads were very clear. 'Because of the great demand for BINKY tickets, only one ticket will be sold per customer.' And we can't hold a place for him in line, either."

"Then he's making a big mistake," said Prunella. "This is one of the most important events of the century."

Rubella did some quick calculations on her chart.

"Arthur has Neptune in Capricorn," she said.

"Is that bad?" asked Francine.

Rubella nodded. "BINKY-wise, he's doomed."

Chapter 2

Arthur was not happy.

He paced back and forth in the shoe store, dragging his feet on the carpet.

"Arthur, stop that," said his mother. "You're going to wear out your new sneakers before we even get out the door."

Arthur turned toward her and folded his arms. "Mom, it took me two minutes to pick these out—120 seconds. I came. I saw. I bought." He frowned. "*What* is D.W.'s problem?"

Mrs. Read sighed. "Your sister," she said, "can be very particular about things."

"I heard that," said D.W., who was

sitting next to a giant pile of shoe boxes. The salesman was wiping his brow while she looked at another pair of sneakers. "These glow in the dark," D.W. explained. "That could be very handy."

"When?" said Arthur.

"You never know," she insisted. "Expect the unexpected, I always say." She looked down. "Hmmmm. It's so hard to decide. The pink high-tops are also nice. Oh, and I don't want to forget the Princess Power moccasins." She poked the salesman. "Have I missed anything?"

The salesman took a deep breath. "I think you've tried on everything we have in your size."

"Come on, D.W.," said Arthur. "Make up your mind. You *do* have one to make up, don't you?"

"Very funny." D.W. wriggled her toes. "These feel pretty good." She smiled at her big brother. "Your problem, Arthur, is that you don't care how you look."

Arthur rolled his eyes. "D.W., they're just sneakers."

"Oh, and I suppose the Bionic Bunny cards you were buying last week were just little pieces of cardboard."

"That was different," said Arthur. "The Bionic Bunny is important. There are collectors all over the country. Some of the cards might be worth a lot of money someday. You need to plan ahead."

"I always plan ahead, except when I don't," said D.W. "You took forever then, and I had to wait for you." D.W. reached for another pair of shoes. "So now *you* can wait for *me*."

It was another five minutes before she finally made her choice. After Mrs. Read paid the bill, the salesman managed a small wave good-bye.

When they got to the car, Arthur opened the door for his mother.

"Such a gentleman," she said.

D.W. laughed. "He's just trying to save time."

Arthur ran around the other side of the car and got in. "I thought they were going to start charging us rent," he said, putting on his seat belt. "Let's hurry, Mom."

As they drove toward the civic auditorium, Arthur groaned. Somehow they were hitting every red light in the universe.

"Put your feet down, D.W." said Mrs. Read.

"Then I can't see my new sneakers as well."

"Never mind that. It's not safe."

As the auditorium came into view, Arthur gasped.

"I knew it! There's a line!"

He pressed his face against the glass.

"That's not a line," said D.W. "That's a whole town. Where's the end of it, anyway?"

That's what Arthur wanted to know. The line seemed to go on forever.

Chapter 3

· · · · · · · · · · · ·

Later that afternoon, everyone was comparing their BINKY tickets at the Sugar Bowl.

"Our seats are all in the front section," said Buster. "Where's yours, Arthur?"

Arthur took out his ticket.

"Row ZZZ."

The other kids all exchanged a look.

"You'll need oxygen up there," said Francine.

"Do you have binoculars?" said the Brain. "Or maybe a telescope."

Arthur just sighed.

Francine looked up at a group photo of BINKY on the wall behind them.

"Wouldn't it be great to meet BINKY?" said Francine. "Not just a handshake — *really* meet them."

"We're just kids," said Arthur. "They probably wouldn't even notice us."

"Maybe not by ourselves," said Buster. "But what if we were with our parents? After all, they're bigger. They stand out more."

Buster was in his living room, serving snacks to Bjorn, Inga, Nero, and Kyra, the members of the group BINKY.

"Cheese curl?" he offered.

"Thanks," said Kyra.

" 'Thanks,' " Mrs. Baxter repeated. She was taking down every word of this historic moment.

"How about a picture?" asked Buster. He took out a camera and aimed it at the group. Everyone smiled.

CLICK!

"Perfect," said Buster. "Just perfect."

"What's perfect?" asked Francine.

"Having a picture of BINKY taken in your own home."

"That would be nice, I suppose," said Francine, "but I know what I'd like even more."

Bjorn, Inga, and Nero were standing outside the civic auditorium. Kyra rushed out to them.

"My priceless sapphire necklace!" she cried. "I think it fell in the trash."

"Call the police!" said Bjorn.

"Call the newspapers!" said Inga

"Call for room service!" said Nero.

The others looked at him strangely.

"Hey, don't blame me," he said. "This is Francine's daydream. And look! Here she comes now."

They turned to see Mr. Frensky's garbage truck speeding up the street. Francine was standing on top, holding out the sapphire necklace.

The truck screeched to a halt in front of the group, and Francine climbed down.

"I believe you lost this," Francine said to Kyra. "My dad found it in the trash and showed it to me. I recognized it right away because you were wearing it last week in that TV interview."

Kyra gave her a big hug. "Whatever can we do to repay you?" she asked.

"Oh," said Francine, "I'm sure we can think of something. . . . Have you ever noticed that groups with five members are even more successful than groups with four?"

"Numbers make a difference," Francine said aloud.

"They certainly do," the Brain agreed.

BINKY's manager opened the door to the biggest office in BINKY World Headquarters.

"We're number one again!" he announced.

The Brain swiveled in his big leather chair. "Yes, yes. Everything is going according to my plan."

"It's amazing how you figured this out," said BINKY's manager. "It was our lucky day when your parents recommended you to me. I mean, I thought we were big before, but your calculations have made us huge."

"Thank you," said the Brain. "I can't say it was nothing because, well, actually it was something."

"And to show our appreciation, we're thinking of renaming the band after you," said the manager.

The Brain smiled. A band called THE BRAIN. It had a nice ring to it.

"You all have the strangest smiles on your faces," said Arthur. "What are you thinking about?"

"Nothing," said Buster.

"It's not important," said Francine.

"Hardly worth mentioning," said the Brain.

But they kept on smiling anyway.

Chapter 4

• • • • • • • • • • •

All the way home, Arthur thought about the upcoming concert. He could tell that his friends were excited about it. He wanted to be excited, too. But with a seat in row ZZZ, excitement seemed as far away as the stage itself.

Nobody at home seemed to realize what a disaster was at hand. Arthur's mother was working on tax returns. His father was making noise in the garage. Kate was taking a nap, and D.W. was watching TV. Arthur could understand about Kate. After all, she was just a baby. But the rest of the family should have been paying attention. This was a crisis. He needed their help.

Arthur wandered into the living room and sat down next to D.W.

"It's not fair," he said.

She didn't answer.

"It's not fair," he said again, this time a little louder.

D.W. kept watching the TV.

"I SAID, IT'S NOT FAIR!" Arthur shouted.

D.W. turned to him. "I heard you, I heard you," she said. "I was just hoping that if I didn't answer, you'd be quiet."

"How can I be quiet when catastrophe is near?"

"How can I watch my show when you keep talking?" D.W. growled.

"It's just the *Sweet Kittens Hour*," said Arthur. "It's not important."

"Oh, really? Like BINKY is such a big deal."

"BINKY is the best!"

"If you say so. But right now I'm in the middle of the show. Can you wait for the commercial?"

Arthur let out a deep breath. "No, I can't wait."

"Well, then go bother Mom. She's just working."

Arthur got up. "That's the only good idea you've had today," he said.

He walked into the dining room and watched his mother from the doorway. She was reading some papers. Every so often she took a pencil from behind her ear and scribbled a correction.

As Arthur watched his mother at work, he was tapped on the shoulder.

"Excuse us," said a voice.

Arthur couldn't believe his eyes. The members of BINKY were waiting to get past him.

"Sorry," he said, moving aside.

The group approached his mother. She didn't

seem surprised. In fact, she looked like she had been expecting them.

"Well," said Mrs. Read, "I have good news and bad news."

"What's the good news?" asked Bjorn.

She smiled. "BINKY is a very successful group."

"And the bad news?" asked Inga.

"You owe a billion dollars in taxes."

Sighing deeply, the group shuffled toward the door, passing Arthur, who was holding out a pen.

"Could I have an autograph?" he asked.

Bjorn sighed. "Not unless you've got a billion dollars to pay for it. "

"Can I help you with something, honey?"

Arthur blinked. His mother was staring at him.

"I think you've done enough," he said. "My seat is terrible, my friends all meet BINKY, and then before I get the chance, you'll scare them back to Finland."

Mrs. Read looked confused. "I will?"

But before she could ask any more questions, Arthur bolted from the room.

Chapter 5

∙ ∙ ∙ ∙ ∙ ∙ ∙ ∙ ∙ ∙ ∙

When Arthur got to class the next morning, he found Buster, Francine, and the Brain deep in conversation. Arthur couldn't help noticing that they were not smiling the way they had been the day before.

"What's the matter?" asked Arthur.

Francine sighed. "We've all been trying to think of a way to meet BINKY," she said. "My dad explained that even though he does collect garbage, he couldn't get near their trash."

"And I was sure my mom would want to interview them for the newspaper," said

Buster. "But she said the entertainment reporter will do that."

"I'm still hoping to think of something," said the Brain. "But so far the situation has resisted my best efforts."

"Now we're just like the other 7,025 kids at the concert," said Francine.

Buster was thinking. "Yes, yes, we are. But that means we still have a chance. After all, we could be the ones they call out of the audience to meet BINKY."

"Does that really happen?" asked Arthur.

"Not always," the Brain admitted. "But it's a statistical possibility."

"You think so?" said Arthur. He smiled. Then there was hope for him, too.

"They can't pick *you*, Arthur," Francine pointed out.

"Why not? I have a seat, too."

"Of course you do," said Francine. "But that's not the problem. What if you were picked? By the time you got to the stage, the concert would be over."

Onstage, BINKY was playing as the audience cheered. Far in the back, with eagles nesting nearby, Arthur was watching the concert through a giant telescope.

The TV entertainment reporter Teena Peters was standing next to him with a microphone. "We're here with Arthur Read," she said. "He has the worst seat ever for a rock concert. What do you think of that, Arthur?"

"Well, I—"

"Wait!" cried Teena, pressing her earpiece. "I've just been told that you've been chosen to meet BINKY in person. Congratulations, Arthur! Go on down!"

Arthur leapt up and ran down the aisle. He ran and ran and ran.

When he finally reached the stage, though, it was empty. Francine and Buster were there to meet him. They looked bigger and older some-

how. Then Arthur caught a glimpse of himself reflected in a mirror. He looked bigger and older, too.

"Where's BINKY?" asked Arthur.

"They're not here," said Francine. "The concert ended three years ago."

"That's how long it took you to get here from your seat," Buster explained.

"But I was running as fast as I could," said Arthur.

Buster pointed to a wheelbarrow stacked high with papers. "Don't worry," he said. "We've saved all your homework assignments."

"Arthur?"

Arthur looked up. Mr. Ratburn was staring at him.

"I don't know where you were, Arthur, but if you don't want to be marked absent, we need your mind here as well as your body."

"Yes, Mr. Ratburn."

Arthur hurriedly took his seat. Clearly, he had a bad case of BINKY-on-the-brain. The problem was, he didn't know if there was a cure.

Chapter 6

• • • • • • • • • • •

That night Arthur sat in his room, staring into the distance.

His father stopped in the doorway. "Want to help me with a job tomorrow night?"

Arthur looked up. "What about the concert? We have to get there early. It will take forever to get to row ZZZ."

"This won't take too long." Mr. Read paused. "I'm catering dinner for the crew working at the civic auditorium."

Arthur frowned. "But that's where we're going for the concert."

Mr. Read tried to look surprised. "Why, that's right. Of course, we can't be out front, then. We'll have to be backstage. The BINKY crew won't eat anywhere else."

Arthur gasped. "The BINKY crew? You? Me? Backstage? I get to go *backstage?*"

His father burst out laughing. "Yes, you do. And when I told the crew my son was such a big fan of the group, they said you could meet BINKY if you want."

"IF I WANT? IF I WANT?" Arthur was jumping around the room.

Mr. Read cleared his throat. "Well, nobody will force you. . . ."

Arthur sighed dreamily. "I'm going to meet BINKY. . . ."

BINKY's manager, Svern Smith, took Arthur's hand and pulled him forward. Flashbulbs were going off all around them. Reporters were shouting out questions in front of a cheering wall of fans.

"This is Arthur Read," said Svern, "a very special boy from Elwood City, here to meet BINKY."

"Hi," Arthur said shyly.

"Hi, yourself," said Nero. "Want to go for a ride?"

They all piled into the official BINKY limousine. Even with the group's instruments, there was plenty of room. Arthur sat in the back, eating cookies and singing.

Suddenly the chauffeur fainted. The limousine veered wildly from one side of the road to the other.

Everyone panicked but Arthur.

"I'll save you!" he cried.

Arthur grabbed a French horn and a rope. He tied one end of the rope to the horn and the other to the armrest. Then he threw the horn out the window. It wrapped around a telephone pole, bringing the limo to a stop right at the edge of a cliff.

Everyone piled out.

"You saved our lives!" said Inga.

"Arthur, you're like the brother we never had," said Nero.

"Come luge with us!" said Kyra.

And so off they went to play in the snow.

Arthur sat in his room, smiling. His father was still there.

"You can bring your friends, too," said Mr. Read. "I'm sure they'd like to meet BINKY, too."

"Really? That's great! Wait until I tell them."

Arthur headed for the hall. He was going to call Buster first. He picked up the phone and started dialing. . . .

Arthur was meeting BINKY again outside their limousine, but this time Buster, Francine, and the Brain were with him.

"My," said Svern, "there's quite a lot of you. We'd take you for a ride, but you wouldn't all fit."

He tossed the kids some BINKY bow ties.
"But at least you can have some souvenirs."

The group got into the car and drove off.

"Wait!" Arthur shouted after them. "You need me to save you. And what about playing in the snow?"

Arthur put down the phone. It was kind of late, and Buster might be asleep or really busy or something. Maybe I won't call just yet, he decided.

Chapter 7

● ● ● ● ● ● ● ● ● ● ●

At school the next day, Arthur looked for a spot to park his bike.

"Over here," said Francine. "I've saved you a space."

"It wasn't easy," the Brain added. "That's a very popular space. But Francine insisted we hold it for you."

"Naturally," said Francine. "Friends should look out for each other, don't you think?"

"Sure," said Arthur.

Buster came pedaling up to them. He looked a bit discouraged.

"One more day," he said. "Then the concert." He sighed. "I'm still trying to get my mother to interview BINKY. Maybe the entertainment reporter will be sick or something. If that happens, I'll get to go."

"I hope it works out," said Arthur.

"You should," said Buster, "because where I go, you all go."

Arthur turned red. "Um, thanks, Buster. It's nice of you to think of us."

Buster shrugged. "Friends should stick together," he said.

When Arthur went inside, Binky called out to him in the hall.

"Hey, Arthur! Wait up!"

Binky sounded excited. Or mad. Sometimes it was hard to tell the difference.

"I've been looking for you," said Binky.

"You have?" Arthur gulped. When Binky went looking for someone, it was usually not a good sign.

"Yeah. You know how the radio station got me in trouble when their staff wrote the BINKY name on everything?"

Arthur remembered. It was the first time he had ever heard of BINKY — a historic date as far as he was concerned.

"Well, the people at the radio station still felt bad about all that confusion. So they sent me three tickets. And since I hear your seat is on the moon or somewhere, I thought you might like to sit with my mom and me."

"Really?" said Arthur. "Gee, thanks."

"No problem. I'm not allowed to sell the ticket, anyway. Besides, I know you'd do the same for me."

"Uh . . . sure." Arthur hesitated. "You know, Binky, it's possible that you could . . ."

Arthur was again standing outside the limousine, this time with Binky beside him.

Svern was making the introductions.

"Binky, this is BINKY . . . and BINKY . . . and BINKY . . . and BINKY. Have I forgotten anyone? Oh, yes, and this is Arthur."

"Your name is Binky?" said Nero.

Binky nodded.

"Then you have to come with us. It must be fate."

Binky and BINKY climbed into the limousine. But when Arthur wanted to climb in after them, he was turned away.

"Sorry, no more room," said Kyra.

The limousine pulled away, leaving Arthur staring after it.

"What about me?" Arthur shouted.

"What *about* me?" said Binky. "Hello? Arthur? I've been standing here forever waiting for you to finish your sentence."

"You have?"

"Yes, you were right in the middle of telling me something. Something that I could do."

"Your homework," Arthur said quickly.

"I was thinking you could do your homework. That is, if you haven't done it already. Which you probably have. But if you haven't, I'd be glad to help."

Binky scratched his head.

"I think I'm all set for now, thanks."

"Okay, then. Oh, I think I hear Mr. Ratburn calling me."

"I don't hear anything," said Binky.

"You really should pay more attention," said Arthur. "I'd better go see what he wants. See you later."

Chapter 8

• • • • • • • • • • •

On the night of the concert, Arthur helped his father prepare the trays of food for BINKY's crew.

"Well, tonight's the big night," said Mr. Read.

"It sure is," said Arthur. But he didn't feel quite as happy about it as he thought he would.

"What kind of plans did you make with your friends?" asked his father. "You know, the security guards won't let them backstage unless I'm with them."

Arthur felt a little uncomfortable. Actually, he felt more than a little uncomfortable. He felt a lot uncomfortable. "Well . . . ," he began, "we didn't really discuss it."

"You didn't?" Mr. Read put down the tray he was holding. "You mean you didn't tell them?"

"It seemed so complicated, Dad. I thought the whole thing might get out of control."

"I see." Mr. Read folded his arms. "And maybe you also decided to keep BINKY to yourself."

Arthur looked at the ground.

"It's your decision, Arthur," said his father, picking up the tray again. "But sometimes when you keep things to yourself, you end up with less than you expected."

When Arthur and his dad got to the civic auditorium, they had to pass an army of security guards. However, Mr. Read had the proper pass, which he wore around his neck. The delicious-smelling food seemed to help, too.

All around them the crew was setting up lights and speakers for that night's performance.

Mr. Read and Arthur were led to a room where a long table was set up. There were some chairs along the wall, too. The room was called the green room, although Arthur couldn't see anything green in it.

As his father uncovered the food, he handed the plastic wrap to Arthur.

"Can you throw this away for me, Arthur?"

Arthur looked around for a trash can. He saw a shiny, silver one and tossed the wrappers inside.

"Watch out, there!"

Arthur jumped back as two stagehands rolled some equipment past him.

"Arthur!"

His father came up behind him with two strangers.

"I want you to meet Winston and Svern," he said. "Winston's in charge of the technical stuff here. Svern is BINKY's manager." Svern and Winston said hi to Arthur and shook his hand. "Arthur's very excited about meeting the group," said Mr. Read.

"Great!" said Svern. "We'll have them up and running in fifteen minutes."

They hurried out.

Arthur frowned. That was odd. They made BINKY sound like some kind of machine. Arthur hoped Svern didn't talk that way in front of the group. He might hurt their feelings.

As Mr. Read unloaded the food trays, Arthur collected the trash and emptied it into the silver cylinder.

Then he snuck out to the stage and peeked out from behind the curtain.

Kids were still pouring into the auditorium. Everyone was talking and having fun. Arthur spotted the whole gang — Francine, Mrs. Frensky, the Brain, Buster, Prunella, Rubella, Sue Ellen, Binky, and Mrs. Barnes — sitting in the front section. Arthur felt a pang of guilt when he saw the empty seat next to Binky.

Arthur went back to the green room and plopped down in a chair. His father gave him a look.

"What's wrong, Arthur?"

"All my friends are here. They're sitting together in the audience."

"Oh, well." His father paused. "So, are you excited about meeting BINKY?"

"I guess so." Arthur sighed. "I thought I would like it better alone. But I was wrong. It would be more fun to share the excitement."

His father smiled. "I'm glad you were able to realize that on your own. As long as that's the case, why not do something about it?"

Chapter 9

• • • • • • • • • • • •

Francine and Buster were craning their necks toward the back row.

"I don't see him," said Francine.

"I knew I should have brought binoculars," said Buster.

"He shouldn't be back there, anyway," said Binky. "I'm saving a seat for him."

"Arthur wouldn't forget a thing like that," said the Brain. "He likes BINKY more than any of us. He'd want to get as close as he could."

"Maybe he got confused," said Francine.

"Or swept away by the crowd," said Prunella.

"If I had a little more room," said Rubella, "I would check his chart again."

"Hi, guys!"

They all turned to see Arthur and his father coming up the aisle.

"Come with us," Arthur said mysteriously. "I have a surprise for you."

"But Arthur," said Buster, "the concert's going to start pretty soon."

"Trust me," said Arthur. "You don't want to miss this."

They followed him backstage, where Svern and Winston were working at the computer console.

The kids looked around in awe.

"That's a Troglibyte 2000," said the Brain, pointing to the console. "It's a very sophisticated piece of equipment. I read about it in *Holographics Today.*"

Svern moved a lever on the computer.

"BINKY is ready!" he announced.

As the stage lights came on behind the closed curtains, the four members of BINKY appeared by their instruments.

"Where did they come from?" asked Francine.

"They weren't here a minute ago," Buster whispered. "Maybe they get some special kind of training so they can sneak past their fans."

Arthur was amazed, too. One moment BINKY hadn't been there, and the next moment they were. He stepped up to Kyra.

"I'm Arthur Read, and these are my friends — Francine, Buster, the Brain, Binky, Prunella, and Rubella. We're very excited to meet you."

Kyra didn't react. She just stood there, staring into space. Arthur swallowed nervously. Had he said the wrong thing somehow? He reached out to shake her hand.

His arm went right through her.

"Whoa!" said Binky.

"Did you see that?" said Francine.

Buster rubbed his eyes.

"Most illuminating," said the Brain.

Svern stepped forward. "It's okay. Really. You see, the members of BINKY aren't real. They're holograms."

Arthur gaped at him.

"I created the images on the Troglibyte 2000," Svern explained. "Winston makes the music."

"Not by myself," Winston added. "I've created a super music synthesizer."

He pointed to a big silver cylinder. Arthur blinked. It looked very familiar.

Winston took a cable and connected the cylinder to Svern's computer.

"We combine my music with Svern's images and . . . *voilà!* BINKY."

Svern pressed a button, and the group started to move and sing. But their mouths

didn't match up with the music. Then Bjorn got stuck on one note that he kept singing over and over again.

"What's going on?" asked Svern.

Winston popped open the top of the cylinder. He pulled out a piece of soggy plastic wrap.

"I think I found the problem," he said.

Chapter 10

● ● ● ● ● ● ● ● ● ● ● ●

Svern peered at the garbage in the super music synthesizer. "Where did all *this* come from?"

"Oops!" said Arthur. "I think I did that. I thought it was a trash can."

Winston started to laugh. "You know, I never saw the resemblance till now." He took the trash out and wiped out the inside.

"Good as new," he said.

Arthur was relieved — and so was everyone else.

Svern glanced at his watch. "Hey, it's

almost showtime! You kids better head back out front or you're going to miss it."

They all hurried to their seats.

"So," said Mrs. Frensky, "did you all get to meet BINKY?"

Francine laughed. "I guess so. Arthur got the closest."

"But they didn't shake his hand," said Buster.

"I'm sure they just had a lot to think about," said Mrs. Barnes. "It was probably hard for them to give you their full attention."

"I'll say," said Prunella.

The others just smiled.

Arthur didn't say anything.

"Well, I like BINKY better this way." said Binky.

"You do?" said Buster. "Why?"

"Because this way I don't have to share my name with real people."

Mrs. Barnes and Mrs. Frensky looked mystified, but the others laughed.

"The Troglibyte 2000 is more powerful than I thought," said the Brain.

"It sure makes me look at celebrities in a whole new way," said Francine.

Arthur nodded. He didn't share the Brain's interest in machines, but he knew one thing for sure: He'd take real friends over a make-believe group any day.

"Ooooh!" cried Prunella as the lights went down.

The curtain was pulled back, revealing Bjorn, Inga, Nero, and Kyra in place with their instruments. BINKY was ready to go.

The audience went wild.

At first, Arthur sat still while the others bounced in their seats. He was still getting used to the idea that the members of BINKY were an illusion. But gradually he found his feet tapping with the music.

Then his arms began to move, and his shoulders, too.

BINKY might not be real, but they still rocked.